MW01206136

LIFE ON THE PORCH SWING

written for seniors
by

Kay Witschen

Illustrated by
Leslie Schumacher

COPYRIGHT © 2007
ALL RIGHTS RESERVED

First Printing 2007

Published by Dwitt Publishing
9249-17th St. S.E.
St. Cloud, MN 56304
Web-site
www.dwittpublishing.com
E-mail: dickawit@aol.com

ISBN
978-0-9741352-3-6

Printed by:
Sunray Printing Solutions, Inc.
25123-22nd Ave.
St. Cloud, MN 56301
E-mail: info@sunrayprinting.com

LIFE ON THE PORCH SWING

written for seniors
by
Kay Witschen

Keep
Swinging
Kay Witschen

IN MEMORY OF

Dorothy Rimer Womeldorf

My Mother,
my teacher,
my friend.

LIFE ON THE PORCH SWING

PROLOGUE

"I don't care if you're my twin sister or not-you're an arrogant stuck up old broad and you do not EVER have to speak to me again."

The sweat was dripping off Emily's brow. She was red in the face, frustrated and angry. *I'm too much of a lady to even answer her, she thought.*

LIFE ON THE PORCH SWING

CHAPTER ONE

Sarah wasn't even as nervous the night before her wedding as she was now, waiting for her twin sister to show up. Another year, another birthday, the *70th* for her and Emily. Last year the celebration had been in New York City, Emily's hometown.

This birthday dinner was being held in Pittsburgh as there was not a restaurant in Sarah's home town of Rimer that was exclusive enough for Emily's taste.

Sarah chose a table by the front window to watch for her sister. She was deep in thought, planning how to bring an idea up to Emily when she saw the long black limo stop in front of the restaurant.

Emily made her grand entrance, looking more like 45 than 70, dressed to the hilt and making Sarah feel like a dowdy old lady.

"Sarah, you look wonderful as always."

"And Emily, you're so full of b.s. as always," laughed Sarah. "But give me a hug; it's way too long since we've seen each other."

After their birthday martinis were ordered they chattered on about old friends they had heard from and caught up on all the usual gossip that was part of the fun. Little did they know that before the dinner was over they would be screaming at each other.

The dinner was wonderful. By the third martini Sarah decided to steer the conversation around to what had been on her mind for weeks.

"Emily, don't you get lonely living alone? Sometimes I feel like there is nothing left for me. Maybe if Ed and I had been able to have the children we hoped to have, things

3

would have been different. You know it was in our plan but he got killed in that accident so soon after we married.."

"I know what you mean about getting lonely. Even with a busy social life, it's not like having a loved one to share every day with. I guess we had never been sure we wanted children because we were not sure they would fit into our life style. I think it was best that we never had any."

"Ladies," said the young waiter, "may I bring you anything else?"

"Not me," replied Sarah. "I've

5

had enough."

"Bring me another drink, you good-looking young man."

"Just one then?" said the red-faced young waiter.

Emily looked disgusted as she said, "O.K., cancel mine and bring the check. My sister is Mrs. Goody-two-shoes and wouldn't THINK of having another."

When the waiter was out of earshot, Emily said, "Sarah, you always were such a damn party-pooper."

"And you, Emily, have always had such a garbage mouth."

Emily laughed. "Sounds like old times."

"Emily, maybe we should try living together."

"WHAT?" yelled Emily.

She thought about it for a few minutes. "That doesn't sound like such a bad idea. Could you get used to living in the big city?"

"Hold on a minute, Emily. What makes you so sure we wouldn't be living right here in good old

Pennsylvania?"

A look of horror was frozen on Emily's face. "Good heavens woman, you can't imagine for one minute that I could go back to living in Podunk, PA, do you?"

"Well excuse me your royal highness. Do you think I would consider living where you do and associate with those high class friends of yours? All they do is stand around having cocktails and looking like they have a stick up their butts."

"Watch your mouth, Sarah. You don't have to be so rude. Besides, don't you have some 'ugh' children living in the house next to you?"

"I don't care if you're my sister or not, you are an arrogant stuck-up old broad and you do not ever have to speak to me again!!!," replied Sarah.

The sweat was dripping from Emily's brow. She was red in the face, frustrated and angry. *I'm too much of a lady to even answer her.*

CHAPTER TWO

They ordered another round of martinis, then another, and finally they were speaking to each other once more.

"If you've got the guts, Sarah, we'll flip a coin to see where we'll live. The loser will promise to stay in that location for one year. At the end of that time we will move to the other location. By the end of that second year we will each be free to make our own choice."

By this time the sisters were feeling the effects of the martinis. "Who's gonna flip the coin?" asked

Sarah.

"I can fix that," said Emily. "Hey waiter, you good looking cutie-pie. We need you over here."

The polite young man tried to hide a smile as he approached the table. "What can I do for you beautiful young ladies?"

"Shut up Emily. I can see that nasty mind of yours at work."

"We just want you to flip this coin for us," said Sarah.

"Do you mind my asking what the toss is for?"

Sarah explained. "Which ever lucky one wins the toss, it will be that house we will share for a year."

"I get heads," shouted Emily.

"Oh, sure—you always get first choice, don't you?"

"O.K. kids, no fighting. Now just give me a coin to toss."

Emily gave the waiter a quarter. The coin went high and spiraled down to the floor.

"There you are," he announced. "Tails is the big winner."

"No," screamed Emily, "this can't be happening. I've changed my mind."

"Oh, I almost forgot what a sore loser you have always been."

"Shut up Sarah. You know that I always keep my word, no matter what."

"Well you better," said Sarah, "and we should leave this place before they throw us out."

"You're right on that," said Emily. "I'll get the chauffer to bring the limo."

CHAPTER THREE

The next day, when the girls were sober and both wondering if this was going to work, they went ahead with the plans.

"Will you rent out your beautiful home, Emily?"

"No. I'll keep the caretaker on for the year until we see how things go. I don't imagine I can survive any longer than that in this awful town."

Not with that attitude, thought Sarah.

Emily returned to New York to

make preparations. The phone line between her home and Sarah's was busy for the next week. After a dozen conversations Sarah finally convinced Emily that NO — she could not bring her own bedroom furniture, fine china or any other household furnishings. By the end of the week Sarah was beginning to wonder if this was the worst idea she ever had.

CHAPTER FOUR

The big day arrived before Sarah was ready. It was pouring down rain when the black limousine pulled up in front of the house. The driver held an umbrella, helped Emily out of the car and brought her to the door.

Sarah quickly ushered them into the living room. The limo driver was looking around the room as if he were in a hovel.

"My heavens, Sarah. Does it rain every day in this forsaken place?"

"Excuse me, Madam," said the

16

driver. "The truck has arrived. Where may I direct the men to put your trunks?"

"A truck! How much stuff did you bring with you? My house is not that big as you well know!"

"Don't worry, Sarah. Just show them your spare room and my bedroom and they'll get the trunks all in."

Sarah showed the movers upstairs and in about six or seven trips up with the trunks they were finished.

Sarah went to the kitchen to put

on the coffee pot and allow Emily privacy to bid goodbye to the limo driver and pay the truck driver and his crew.

The sisters sat in the kitchen and had coffee and fresh home baked cookies that Sarah had prepared.

"I suppose you are making this EVIL fat food all the time, Sarah."

"I guess I am," laughed Sarah. "Part of the reason is that I like to have a treat for the twins next door."

"And you just know, my dear sister, how NOT thrilled I am to visit with children."

18

"I think you have a bad attitude towards kids just because neither one of us was lucky enough to have any," replied Sarah.

"Let's not discuss this any further, please."

"You may just change your mind when you meet them. Anyway, this has been a long day and I am off to bed."

"You and me both," said Emily. "See you in the morning, but not very early."

CHAPTER FIVE

Sarah was up early the next day, had coffee on and had no idea what her sister liked for breakfast. It was another hour until Emily made her appearance.

"Sarah, do you get up with the chickens every day?"

"Yes, I guess I do. I never got in the habit of sleeping late. I got up early for work until two years ago and after retirement I couldn't seem to sleep longer in the morning."

"Don't expect to see me any earlier," laughed Emily.

"That's just fine. Now what do you like for breakfast? Anything more than coffee, you're free to serve yourself."

"Just toast for me," said Emily.

"Great. That's what I have in the morning but it has to be piled high with apple butter."

"Oh, Sarah. Do you remember when Mom and those neighbor women made apple butter in that huge iron kettle over an open fire in the backyard?"

"Yes I certainly do. I can remember how we had to take turns with them stirring with that big wooden paddle."

Other memories of their childhood slipped in as the sisters drank a pot of coffee and enjoyed each other's company.

"Let's go out and enjoy your porch swing and this beautiful weather," said Emily.

CHAPTER SIX

"I guess I have to admit that I don't get this kind of peace living where I do," said Emily.

Sarah laughed, "I think you and I and most of our friends figured out what life was all about while swinging on the porch. Or at least what we thought life, sex and marriage were all about."

"Yes," said Emily, "and most of it wasn't quite the way we pictured it."

"Do you remember how angry the girl that lived across the street from us was when she was entertaining her boyfriend on their front porch and we giggled and pointed at them every time he put his arm around her?"

"I guess we were brats," laughed Emily. "Well so much for the old days. There's something I wanted to ask you. What kind of recreation do you enjoy?"

"I wanted to talk with you about that, Emily. How about if we take turns suggesting activities?"

"How often? A major activity? What if the other one disapproves?"

"Suppose something special once a month. The other one of us is under a strong obligation to agree. Also—the one doing the suggesting pays all expenses."

"Well now, Sarah, that doesn't sound bad. How will we decide who gets to be the first to choose?"

"How about the good old coin toss?"

Emily laughed. "Sure, you think you're going to be lucky again."

"Actually I do, but you can do the toss."

"I'll agree to that but let's relax today and take care of the toss tomorrow."

It WAS a relaxing morning. Dan and Megan, twins from next door came over when they saw the women on the porch swing. Sarah could easily tell that her sister was less than pleased to see the kids.

"Dan and Megan, this is my twin that I've told you about several times."

"Oh, hello. So glad to meet you," said Megan.

"Miss Sarah told us about all the

fun you had together when you were young," said Dan.

Emily, well mannered as always, was pleasant to the twins.

"Miss Sarah, did you tell us that your sister was the one that always got the two of you in trouble?"

"Oh, is that so! Maybe I need to visit with you when Miss Sarah's not around," said Emily.

The children laughed. "What do we call you?" asked Dan.

"I guess Miss Emily will be fine."

"Any chance anyone is hungry for chocolate chip cookies this morning?" asked Sarah.

Big smiles were all the answer the eleven-year-olds needed for Sarah to go to the kitchen and come back with cookies and milk.

CHAPTER SEVEN

"Good morning sleepy head. I was afraid you would think I deserted you. A quick walk for a half-hour is pretty usual for me most mornings."

"Sounds terrible, Sarah. I usually get on my treadmill for twenty minutes. Never this early in the day, though. I guess I'll have to change my ways a bit but right now I need coffee."

"I'll have a cup with you. Remember we have a pretty important coin toss to do this morning."

After a few cups of coffee Emily was ready to get down to business. "What special coin do we have to toss?"

"Let's just toss a shiny new penny—this year's date," replied Sarah. "I'll get one out of the coin bank that's sitting on my dresser."

"Here you go, sis. Good Luck!"

Emily chose heads—tossed the coin—which hit the kitchen floor on edge, spun around and ended up sliding under the refrigerator.

"No-o" screamed Emily. "I know it must have been heads."

31

"Well I don't know that—so I'll get another coin but I think we better go to the living room and let it land on the carpet."

"That's fine," said Emily, "but I still get heads."

The second toss landed heads up and Emily couldn't have been happier.

"I'm afraid to ask you, Emily, but what is this month's wonderful activity going to be?"

"There are a few phone calls I need to make before I can tell you."

CHAPTER EIGHT

Later the same day Emily came out to join Sarah on the swing. "Well, I can tell you the activity but it has to be postponed until next month. Looks like you'll get the first one after all. My activity will be an ocean cruise, Sarah, lasting five days."

"Oh good heavens. I don't know if I can do that without getting sick and I don't have dressy clothes and I think it will cost you too much money and…"

"Take a breath, Sarah. I'll buy you the proper clothes. They give patches to put on your arm to prevent sea sickness. And you know without me saying it that I'm loaded with money. I'm not bragging—it's just the way it is."

"I'm aware of that, Emily. We'll talk about that another time. I'm living a very comfortable life with pensions, insurance money and savings. Since I'm going to be doing the planning of the first activity then, we'll get started on it tomorrow."

"Aren't you going to tell me what it is?"

"No, Emily. I'll just surprise you."

CHAPTER NINE

"I'll do the cooking tonight, Sarah. I think it would be fair if we took turns, don't you?"

"Sounds fine with me. Then we can take life easy this evening for tomorrow will be a very special shopping trip."

"Oh, great! I love to shop. Where are we going?"

"It's probably better if you find that out tomorrow, Emily."

Chicken breasts with rice and smothered with a cheese sauce along with a salad was soon on the table.

"I'm impressed. I had no idea you were such a great cook. It really is a treat to have dinner prepared by someone else right here at home."

"I hope you saved room for this strawberry shortcake."

"I think I can manage that just fine, Emily."

The next morning Sarah couldn't wait for Emily to get up and ready for their shopping trip. She had the list of things they would be needing all prepared, thanks to a book she had checked out from the library a week before Emily's arrival.

Finally a sleepy looking Emily came down the stairs, still wearing her bathrobe.

"I hope you don't mind if I'm dressed like this when I have breakfast."

"What I would like is for you just to feel at home. You are free to do what you choose. Whenever you're ready we'll head for downtown."

An hour later the girls were on their way. When Sarah parked the car in front of a sports store, Emily said "what in the world are we coming here for?"

"Just wait. You'll see."

"How can I help you young ladies?" asked the salesman.

"We need to get fitted with on-line skates and all the necessary equipment. I believe that would be helmets, knee pads, elbow pads and wrist guards."

"Sounds like you know what you're doing."

"NO, she does not! Sarah, have you lost your mind?"

"Now Emily, a deal is a deal."

CHAPTER TEN

"Megan, come quick. You won't believe this."

Megan ran to her brother's side to see what had him peering through the slit in the backyard fence.

"Move over, Dan and let me see what's going on."

Dan moved aside, still not able to believe what he was seeing.

"Miss Sarah and Miss Emily are trying on ROLLER BLADES. I don't believe it. They'll kill themselves."

"Shh, Megan. I'm trying to hear what they are saying."

"Now listen, Sarah. This is another of your hare-brained ideas that will do nothing but get us in trouble or get us killed."

"Emily, if we weren't twins I would think you were twenty years older than me because you never want to have any fun."

"Megan," whispered Dan, "they ARE going to try those skates."

"Let me get a better look, Dan," said Megan as she squeezed in closer to the opening. " It looks like they have quite a pile of equipment there."

"Emily, now think about this. We bought everything we need for a safe tryout right here on our own driveway. What more do we need?"

"Just brains, Sarah. Just good old fashioned horse sense."

"Here Emily. I borrowed a book from the library that tells us everything we need to know to begin in-line skating. Just look at the illustrations. If we learn the basics today of how to get going, that will be a good day's work."

"I think learning how to stop before we start would be a better idea, Miss smarty-pants."

"Dan, what are we going to do? They could really get hurt."

"I don't want them to know we were spying on them. Let's check when we come back from the ball game and see how they are doing."

CHAPTER ELEVEN

Dan and Megan went immediately to the backyard fence when they returned from their game but all was quiet.

"Their lights are out. They must be in bed," said Megan.

"Good. Maybe they gave up the skating idea. I hope so. I would hate to see anything happen to either of them."

The next morning, long before Dan and Megan were up, the sisters were outside getting ready for their first attempt at skating.

"You know Emily, we did lots of skating at the old skating rink when we were teenagers and we were good at it."

"May I point out a small difference sister dear. It is true that these skates have four wheels. I know our old skates also had four wheels. It just so happens, due to positioning and weight distribution, you were not probably going to fall on your face the minute you tried to stand up on the old ones."

"Well la-te-da Miss well

informed. Just look at this picture in the book. We should try this first on the grass, walking with our toes pointed out like a duck walk."

"That's just fine, Sarah. You go right ahead and try it. I give you my permission to start without me."

"Emily, quit being such a pessimist and let's get suited up."

Dan and Megan were having breakfast when they heard a strange noise.

"It's coming from next door, Dan. Let's take a look."

They hurried out the back door to the space in the fence where they saw a disgruntled Emily sitting on the ground, howling as though she were in pain.

The children dashed around the fence and ran to the sisters.

"Miss Emily, are you alright?" asked Dan.

"Well young man, I sure have had better days. If you want to know who got me into this mess, just ask Miss Know-it-all Sarah. She bought all this equipment but it seems to me she forgot a padded seat. Here children, help me up. I don't think

I could possibly do it by myself."

"Miss Emily," said Megan, "this is the easiest way to get back up." Megan sat down on the ground beside Miss Emily and went through the motions, showing her to kneel on one knee and then push up to a standing position.

"Thank you, Megan. And as for you, Sarah, I'm done for today. If you want to break your fool neck then just be my guest."

At that point the children returned home, hoping that Emily would talk Sarah out of the whole idea.

Despite her protests, Emily did keep trying until by noon both sisters were able to make it to the end of the sidewalk and back. A little shaky but upright.

CHAPTER TWELVE

A few days later, Dan and Megan were at the park with their friends, talking about a race that was going to be part of the summer festival activities. It was to be sponsored by the town council and was open to in-line skaters of all ages.

"We can't skate against high school kids," said Jeff.

"Why not?" asked Megan. "We skate as well as they do. Maybe better."

"That's not the point," said Dan.

"They have the advantage because their legs are so much longer. Anyway, I think the race is to have three categories: 9 and under, then 10-14, which is us of course, and 14 and over."

"The race will be held next Saturday. I can hardly wait. This should be a blast. Let's go get a set of rules and sign-up sheets from the city clerk," said Tara.

CHAPTER THIRTEEN

Emily and Sarah spent the next couple of days practicing in the driveway.

"Sarah, I have to admit this is fun, as long as we take it easy and just stay close to home."

"Well, Emily, it's about time you admit that you're having a good time. If you just listened to me more often we could do such wonderful things. Just think, we could…."

"Sarah, shut up!"

"Well, EXCUSE ME!"

Dan and Megan stopped to see the sisters on their way home from the park.

"Hi," Megan called. "Looks like you two are getting pretty good at this."

"Only as long as we take it easy," said Emily. "We just have to recognize our limits."

"Oh Emily. We have no limits except in your head."

"We baked your favorite cookies this morning. Maybe if you joined us for some cookies and milk Sarah would let me take a break."

"All right," laughed Dan. "You don't have to ask us twice."

As they sat on the porch enjoying the snack with the sisters, Dan told them about the race that was scheduled for Saturday.

"We're practicing our skating too," said Megan. "Dan and I will be skating as a team."

"They have some really neat prizes," said Dan. "We think we have a pretty good chance at winning. There's only one really bad spot in the route they have mapped out."

"Where's that?" asked Sarah.

"It's Baker's hill that comes right into the middle of town. It's so steep and even though traffic will be blocked off, there are still people walking who don't watch where they're going. I'm always afraid of running into someone."

"Dan, we better get home or we'll be late for supper. Hope we see you two at the festival," said Megan as she waved goodbye.

"Emily, I notice you don't seem to think kids are so bad since you met Dan and Megan."

"You don't have to rub it in. Yes I think they are very special."

"I think we should go and watch the race and cheer them on to victory," said Sarah.

"Maybe so. As long as we are only going to watch."

CHAPTER FOURTEEN

When the day of the summer festival arrived, Dan and Megan were up early, anxious to get going and wanting to be sure they didn't miss anything.

"Okay you two. Sit down at the table and eat a decent breakfast before you leave."

"Aw, Mom, we're in a hurry. We can eat something when we get downtown," said Dan.

"That's exactly why you're going to eat before you go. I can imagine what junk food you'll be finding at the festival. At least I want to know that you started the day with a healthy breakfast."

Megan looked at Dan and rolled her eyes as she resigned herself to sitting down at the table and doing what their Mother asked.

After finishing breakfast they each gave their Mother a quick hug as they headed for the door.

"What time will you be skating?"

"Around two o'clock, Mom. Are you and Dad coming to watch?" asked Dan.

"We wouldn't miss it! We'll see you both later—in the winner's circle," she said with a smile.

CHAPTER FIFTEEN

Emily and Sarah were having a discussion over breakfast that came close to no longer being a discussion but started sounding more like an old-fashioned argument.

"Of course we're going to the festival, Sarah, just like you've done for the past 24 years—ever since the town started HAVING a festival but we are NOT going there on skates, trying to act like we're teen-agers."

"Emily, sometimes you make me downright disgusted. Don't you ever like to do something different? You old stick-in-the-mud!"

"Let me tell you this Miss Sarah know-it-all. What I don't like is making a complete fool of myself." And with that, Emily got up from the table, slammed the screen door and went to sit on the front porch.

CHAPTER SIXTEEN

Emily had been sitting alone on the front porch for nearly an hour before Sarah joined her.

"Okay, Emily, we'll do it your way—no skates. I don't want you to be angry with me. I guess I just like to keep moving fast enough so old age won't catch me too quickly."

"I think it's me that's wrong, Sarah. Let's do it—let's put on our skates and get up town and if anyone laughs at us—so be it."

"No, Emily, we'll do it your way."

"We will NOT," replied Emily in a louder than usual voice.

Sarah knew it was time to stop getting Emily riled up. She smiled and said quietly, "let's get ready so we're in plenty of time to watch Dan and Megan."

CHAPTER SEVENTEEN

Sarah drove the car downtown and found a good parking space near the city park.

"We'll leave our skates in the car for now while we have lunch and find out where the starting point is for the races."

As they looked around at different booths and novelty stands, Dan and Megan came by.

"Hi," they called as they skated toward the sisters. "Are you going to watch the race?" asked Dan.

"We wouldn't miss it for anything."

"If you can get over to Baker Street, that's probably the best place to watch as it's almost the end of the race. We will be lined up and starting about two o'clock, so you should be there by that time as the whole course goes fast—probably fifteen minutes at the most. Well, wish us luck," Dan added as he and Megan skated off.

"We do, we do," called the sisters in unison.

CHAPTER EIGHTEEN

After lunch the sisters made their way back to the car, gathered up their skates and all the gear and sat down at a bench to get suited up. It seemed as though the whole town had turned out for the celebration. A number of strange looks were cast at the sisters but they were so busy getting on their pads, etc. that they didn't even notice.

As they started out slowly from the bench, Emily was more than a little nervous.

"Sarah, maybe we should just...."

"Come on Emily, just loosen up and you'll be fine. You have been doing great on the sidewalks by the house."

"But Sarah, people are looking at us in a very peculiar way."

"Come on now. Maybe they just wish they knew how to skate," Sarah replied as she gave Emily her hand for a few minutes to steady her as they went along.

CHAPTER NINETEEN

It took about twenty minutes for the sisters to get over near the best viewing area at Baker Street. The number of people on the street and sidewalks even had Sarah nervous but she was not about to let Emily know that.

"I think we got over here just in time, Emily. I heard the starting gun for the race. Megan and Dan should be coming this way before long."

"I wish we had a place to sit down," said Emily. "That was pretty tiring."

"Let's just edge our way out through the crowd so we can see a little better. After the race we can sit and rest. I'm bushed too," admitted Sarah.

As they made their way through the crowd they heard the cheers and realized the skaters were coming close. The crowd moved in closer and closer and all of a sudden Emily felt herself being pushed further and further out into the street. Skaters were flying by and she couldn't hold steady. She was starting to move downhill and couldn't stop.

"Emily, Emily," she could hear Sarah shouting. "Put on your

brakes."

It wasn't working, as the people intent on watching the skaters were thrusting her forward.

Sarah fought her way to the street in time to see an unsteady Emily on her way down the hill, out of control. She knew she had to try to catch her so she pushed forward and started her decline.

Megan and Dan were in third place, gaining steadily on the two teams ahead when they spotted Emily.

"Oh, no," yelled Megan. "It

can't be. We've got to catch her before she kills herself. Let's try to go one on each side and slow her down."

Megan and Dan slowed down even though they both knew that any chance they had of winning the race was gone. By the time they were able to each grab one of Emily's arms she was barely able to stand.

Sarah had almost caught up and was skating down the hill behind them, so thankful the kids had caught Emily for she knew she would never have been able to keep her from falling.

"LOOK

OUT,"

yelled

Dan,

74

but it was too late. A man ran out into the street directly in front of the trio and there was no way they could avoid hitting him. As all four crashed to the pavement a bag the man was carrying flew open and money was flying in every direction. Just as the man was struggling to get to his feet, Sarah in hot pursuit of the trio, knocked him down once more.

Suddenly sirens were screaming and police cars were everywhere. An alarm inside the bank had been activated in plenty of time to allow the police to get there soon enough to take the culprit into custody. Emily and Sarah were soon on their way to the hospital by ambulance.

CHAPTER TWENTY

A few hours later the sisters were resting comfortably in a hospital room, suffering minor cuts and a large amount of bruising.

"Emily will you ever forgive me?"

"Aw, Sarah, it was probably one of the most exciting days of my life. And just think of the reward the bank is giving us for taking care of that bank robber for them."

Headlines in the morning paper read:

BANK ROBBER FOILED BY SKATERS

A courageous brother and sister forfeited their chance to win a race in order to save their neighbors. A bank robber was tripped up in the middle of his getaway by Dan and Megan Woodley as they were assisting Emily Simpson and Sarah Hadley to the bottom of Baker's hill. A grateful town has showered the foursome with gifts and reward money is forthcoming from the bank.

A celebration featuring an enormous cake (with in-line skaters decorating the top) and gallons of ice cream was held by the town to honor the sisters and Dan and Megan.

"What are you folks going to do with that reward money?" asked a reporter.

"All of it is going into a college fund for Dan and Megan, who no doubt were the real heroes of the day," said Sarah.

"What are you sisters going to do for excitement now?" continued the reporter.

"Just take a nice long rest," said Emily. "Maybe somewhere nice and sunny."

"I know the perfect place," said Sarah. "And while we're there, maybe along with just lounging on the beach, we could take some para-sailing lessons."

"Sarah, don't you even think about it," said Emily as she shook her fist.

The whole group was laughing.

"Just kidding, Emily."

CHAPTER TWENTY ONE

It took only two weeks until the sisters were back to normal, bruises were gone, cuts all healed.

"You know, Sarah, I've been thinking about the cruise I have booked for us. I'm going to change it to a different trip."

"Oh, dear. I was so hoping that maybe you had forgot about it. Well, what are you cooking up now?"

"I'm going to book a cruise that is just for singles. I think there are a lot of single men around the same age as we are that get lonesome for women to talk with, have dinner with, dance with, etc."

"Please don't do that, Emily. You know I'm not very out-going. The talking, the dinner, maybe the dancing, doesn't sound so bad, it's the ETC. that scares me."

Emily started laughing. "Well honey, after what you put me through on those skates, the choice is definitely mine and a singles cruise it will be!"

"Just so you know. I'm taking a dozen books to read with me, smarty pants, and I just may stay in my room or cabin or whatever you call it."

"We'll see, honey. In any event, tomorrow we shop and the next week we will be cruising."

THE END

AUTHOR

Kay Witschen grew up in Rimersburg, PA. She met and married Dick Witschen in San Diego when they were both in the Marine Corps. At the end of their service time they returned to Dick's hometown, St. Cloud, MN.

They have spent the winters for the last several years in San Juan, TX, enjoying time as "winter Texans."

ILLUSTRATOR

Leslie Schumacher is a central MN artist. She also serves as the executive director for the Central MN Arts Board, one of eleven regional arts councils serving the state of MN.

CHILDREN'S BOOKS BY KAY WITSCHEN
For preschool thru age 8

CLINKER'S FLEA
(1998 Out of Print)
CLINKER'S SHADOW
1999
CLINKER MEETS THE FLYING SQUIRREL
2001
CLINKER'S CHRISTMAS STAR
2004
CLINKER'S DRAGON
2006

For age 8 thru 11

JOHNNY COALBOY
2003